TALES OF

The Legend of Joseph Daw

GERARD RONAN

Illustrated by Derry Dillon

libraries.
fingal.ie

Text copyright © by Gerard Ronan 2021
Illustration copyright © by Derry Dillon 2021

Cover designed by Derry Dillon.

Photograph of gibbet - The Miriam and Ira D. Wallach Division of Art, Prints and Photographs: Photography Collection, The New York Public Library. "Gibbet used in St. Vadier near Quebec in 1763 for the body of Mdme. Dodier hung for murder of her husband. Exhumed in 1850 and sold to the Boston Museum theater and after that was given up-sent to the Essex Institute." The New York Public Library Digital Collections. 1860 - 1920.
https://digitalcollections.nypl.org/items/510d47d9-bf49-a3d9-e040-e00a18064a99

Gerard Ronan asserts his moral right to be identified as the author of this work in accordance with the Irish Copyright and Related Rights Act 2000.

All rights reserved. No part of this publication may be copied, reproduced, stored in a retrieval system, broadcast or transmitted in any form or by any means, electronic, mechanical, photocopying, recording or otherwise without prior permission in writing from the author.

This novel is a work of fiction. Any references to real people or real events are used solely to lend the fiction an appropriate historical setting. Names, characters, businesses, places, events, locales, and incidents are either the products of the author's imagination or used in a fictitious manner. Any resemblance to actual persons, living or dead, or actual events is purely coincidental.

ISBN: 9781914348006

A CURIOUS ENCOUNTER

I HAVE NEVER been much of a person for telling ghost stories. It's not that I don't believe in ghosts, it's more that I find the telling of such tales to be tiresome and so far from my own experience of the poor creatures as to make a mockery of their suffering.

That being said, I find myself getting old and in possession of a story that you are free to believe, or disbelieve, as you see fit. I am telling this story because I am fast approaching my seventy-sixth birthday and it's high time I told somebody.

It all began on a sunny Wednesday afternoon in 1934. I remember the day particularly well because it was the day after May Day and a news item that had been broadcast on the wireless that morning had enraged my father.

We were neither of us, my father and I, much given to conversing at the breakfast table, and so, to kill the silence my mother would frequently turn on the wireless. To her it was like a fourth member of the family; a chatterbox or conversation starter that made the house feel more alive and her domestic chores a little less solitary.

Well, that particular morning, during the eight o'clock news, it was announced that the Irish government intended to refuse an application from the deposed Russian leader, Leon Trotsky, to come and live in Ireland. My father was livid. Dad, you see, was a member of the Irish Communist Party, which was quite a trendy thing to be back then, and he had been looking forward to the possibility of meeting the great Leon Trotsky in person.

Dad never won many friends on account of his socialist beliefs and, though I didn't always agree with him, I was always proud of the fact that he was a little bit different from other dads. Indeed, had I been blessed with half of his courage I might well have written this story years ago. But I wasn't. I was too afraid of the consequences, afraid to stand out from the crowd.

Anyway, as I was saying, it was a Wednesday, a school day, and a working day, and as soon as Dad had left for the docks, where he worked as a stevedore, and I'd been packed off to school, Mam intended to catch a train to Balbriggan to visit her parents. All of these things are important, for had even one of them failed to coalesce that particular day, the house would not have been empty that afternoon and I would not have this story to tell.

The day may have started badly, with Dad leaving for work in foul humour, a mood that was likely to last the entire day, but it was also in some ways a lucky day – at least for me if not for poor Trotsky. That afternoon, the headmaster decided to call an emergency teachers' meeting and we were let out early from school. It could never happen now, of course, but things were far more relaxed back then and teachers were not always as sane, or as saintly, as they are today.

As my parents did not know I was going to be let out early from school, I knew that there would be no one at home. And so, with time on my hands and no homework to do, I decided to indulge myself, and go exploring.

Heading down the Beaverstown Road, I climbed the wall of Lamb's orchard and, under the cover of the fruit trees, made my way out to the marshy shores of the Rogerstown Estuary. From here I began to follow the shoreline in the direction of Butler's Meadow, where the Ballough River narrowed to a meandering brook and fish could be more easily seen, and caught. Yes, you read that correctly. There were fish in the river back then, and you wouldn't get sick if you drank the water. How times have changed, eh?

As a child, I loved to be out in the wilds of the estuary. You could see herons, hares, and oystercatchers out on the salt marshes, and in summer large mobs of linnets would sweep about the sky, turning and twisting like dark clouds in a gusting wind. It was, still is, a magical sight to behold.

I say 'mobs' or 'clouds' of linnets, of course, because that's how they appeared to me back then and those were the only words I could think of to describe them. I have recently discovered, however, that the collective noun for linnets is 'parcel'. A 'parcel' of linnets, you're supposed to say, and a 'murder' of crows. Crazy, isn't it?

But I digress again, a recently acquired habit, a curse that comes with old age. But please bear with me, for I need to tell you of another of my youthful passions – foxes. And this time I do not digress, for it was a fox that led me to the spot where the incident took place.

Whenever I went exploring on the estuary, I would always keep a weather eye open for paw prints, for I lived in the eternal hope of one day finding an abandoned cub. I haven't seen a fox on the peninsula since the 1990s, but they were a common sight back then, and an orphaned fox cub was every young boy's dream pet.

Well, as it happened, that afternoon, I chanced to come upon a set of fresh prints and attempted to follow them. You can tell a fox's print from that of a dog by the way, by the larger gap between the pads. Did you know that? No matter, what is important is that I knew it to be a fox and not a dog and that I became so engrossed in tracking him that I lost track of time. By the time I realised it was getting late, the tide had come in.

Looking behind me, I could see that the track I'd followed was slowly being covered by water. If I retraced my steps my feet would get soaked and my father would thrash me good-oh for ruining my school shoes! No, going back the way I'd come simply wasn't an option.

The safest, and driest route, I quickly

decided, would be to follow the fox prints inland and towards Daw's Bridge; a tiny stone bridge that lay between Turvey Hill and Blake's Cross on the old Drogheda Road.

There was a gate on that road that could easily be climbed, and from there I knew that I could walk safely home along Turvey Avenue. The entire detour would take no more than an extra twenty minutes. I'd be late for supper, but at least I would be dry. And that, dear reader, is exactly what I did.

I was just yards from the stone bridge when first I saw it, hanging from a leafless tree on the southern side of the stream. It was difficult to make it out at first, but the closer I got, the more it began to look like a cage; a cage with a dark shape inside it. Indeed I was almost on top of it before I recognized the shape to be that of a man.

'Hallo there,' he shouted. 'Pray tarry young

sir, and be not afraid. Take pity on a poor wretch. I'll not detain you long.'

I hesitated for a second and then, as I turned to continue on my journey, I stumbled on a tuft of grass. As I picked myself up, the caged figure called again.

'Wait, I beg of you,' he said. 'Please! Spare me a moment of your time. It is a matter of the greatest importance. I know that you can see me because I can see you. Fear not, young sir, I cannot harm you, and it may well be in your power to perform a great kindness for a wretched and friendless stranger.'

He was a young man – late twenties or early thirties – and dressed in rags. I found myself strangely intrigued by his manner of speech. There was something ancient about it, something almost biblical.

'What are you doing in there?' I asked.

'That, young sir, is a long story,' he said, as

I tried in vain to place his accent. 'But pray tell, sir, are you by chance travelling in the direction of Swords?'

'Afraid not,' I said. 'Heading for Donabate, and if I'm late for tea Dad will kill me.'

'Then I'll not detain you a moment more than is necessary,' said the caged man. 'My name is Daw, Joseph Daw. And you, young sir, might I have your good name?'

'Billy,' I said. 'Billy Hand. That's Daw's Bridge over there. Did you build it?'

'No Billy, I did not,' he said. 'But it *is* named after me. Tell me, Master Billy, be there a Catholic priest residing yet at the village church in Ballymadrough?'

'There's no village at Ballymadrough,' I laughed, 'and no church that I know of. At least not anymore.'

'Gone!' he sighed sadly. 'Is it truly gone?'

I nodded.

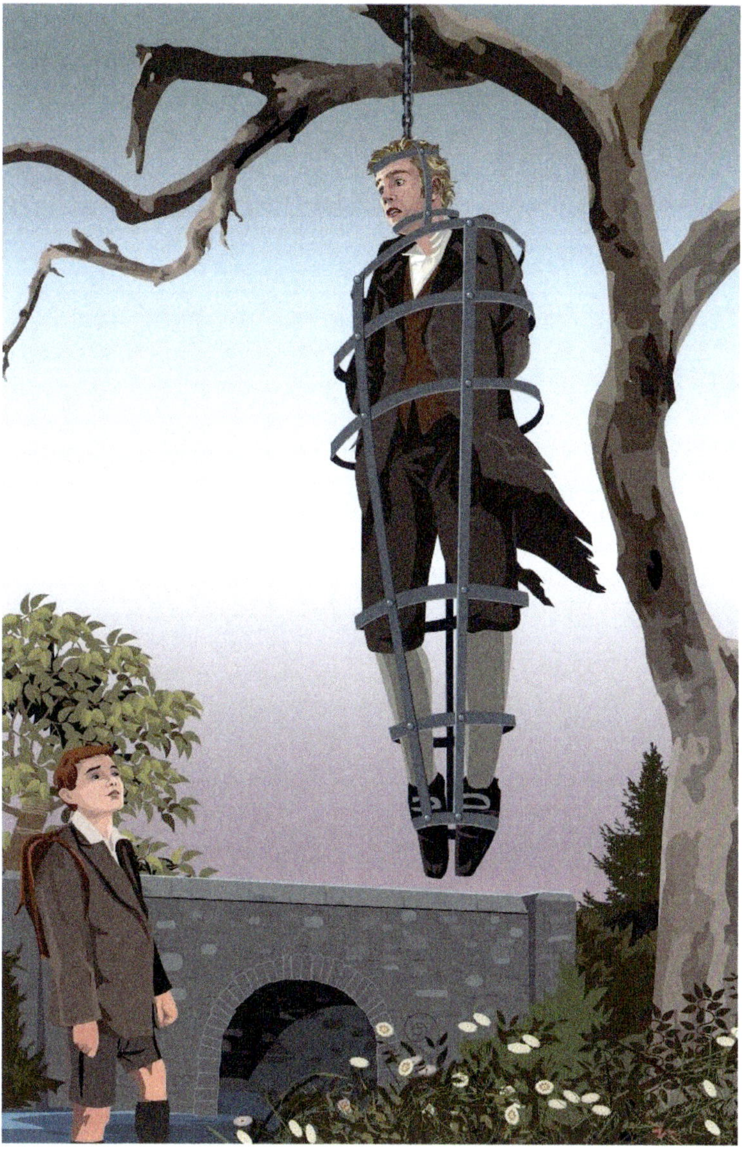

'Pray remind me, Master Billy,' he then enquired, 'what year of our good Lord be this?'

'1934,' I said. 'Don't you know? How come you don't know the year? *Everybody* knows the year!'

He paused for a moment, as if struggling with some mental calculation or other, and then, ignoring my questions, proceeded to ask another of his own.

'And where might the nearest priest be now?' he inquired softly. 'The nearest Roman priest, that is.'

'Donabate,' I replied. 'There's a Roman Catholic church and priest's house there. Why do you ask?'

'Because, young sir, I do desperately desire that a message be taken to one and that he be acquainted with my story.'

'You're not from around here,' I then remarked, oblivious to the sadness in his voice, 'and you talk funny. That's an English accent you've got, isn't it? I know it's not Irish.'

'Faith, young sir, but you are observant,' said Daw. 'And yes, you speak true. I was born in the city of Liverpool but I grew to a man not very far from this very spot. Now, pray attend, Master Billy, for I would acquaint you with a story and beg of you to tell it to a priest, and tell it, mind, exactly as I tell it to you. Do you think you could perform this kindness for me?'

'I can try,' I said.

'Then tell him,' he said, 'that Joseph Daw wants a Christian burial or some service of forgiveness to be held at this accursed site.'

'Are you dying?' I asked.

'In a manner of speaking,' said Daw. 'Been that way for the longest time now.'

'Go on then,' I said, curiosity having gotten the better of me and all thoughts of getting home having slipped from my mind.

But I will let Joseph tell you his story now, exactly as he told it to me, or as close as I can remember it after all these years. It is, after all, his story to tell. You can decide for yourself just how much, or how little of it, you want to believe.

JOSEPH DAW'S STORY

My name, as by now you are most probably aware, is Joseph Daw, and I was born of a decent Lancashire family in the year of our Lord 1747. The only child of my parents, I was but four years of age when I lost them, or, more truthfully, had them taken cruelly from me.

We were sailing from Liverpool to Dublin because my father, a master brewer, had been offered employment at a thriving brewery in the city of Dublin, a position that promised a higher standard of living than we at that time enjoyed in Liverpool. Being not of the wealthiest class, we sailed as deck passengers aboard the merchant ship *Rebecca*, a state of affairs that meant we were at all times exposed to the piercing wind and the stinging spray. But we were sailing, or so we believed, to a better life, and so were resolved to endure it.

Only the gentry could afford cabins, and though I mind not admitting to you now that I was sinfully envious of their wealth on that bitter voyage, I would never have voiced such thought to my parents. They were good people, devout Catholics who expected the highest standards of me. Even at four years of age, I understood that, though perhaps time has exaggerated their goodness in my mind, in much the same way as the naming of yonder bridge has exaggerated my sinfulness in the minds of others.

Well, it came to pass, as we neared the Irish coast, that our ship had the grave misfortune to run into a fog so thick that you could see not more than twenty yards ahead. Crashing waves could be heard close by, but they could not be seen, nor could any man on board give a true estimate of how close they might be. But then, all of a sudden, and at the height of the general anxiety, a hopeful shout went up.

'Stern lantern ahead!'

A stern lantern, my father explained, was the lamp that was hung at the back of a ship to prevent other ships from crashing into it in poor visibility. The light appeared to be heading away from us.

'She's lighting our path,' said my father, pointing towards the light. 'See how gently the lantern rises and falls. That could only mean one thing. The ship before us has encountered calmer waters. An estuary, or a river perhaps.'

We never found those calmer waters, for in our attempts to follow the light before us, we ran aground on a sandbar. As the hull hit the bottom, the ship jerked so violently that one of her timbers gave way. Water flooded the hold and the ship began to list.

Everything happened so swiftly after that, that there was not even time enough to launch the ship's lifeboat. In fear for our lives, Mother gathered me into her arms and Father ushered us towards the ship's rails. All about us, there rose a terrible and frantic hullabaloo, and the general expectation was that the ship was about to capsize. There was nothing that could be done. It was every man and woman for themselves.

My father looked gravely at my mother. 'He can barely swim,' he shouted above the screams of the other terrified passengers, 'and I can't… you know… not the both of you.'

'Then take Joseph,' said my mother, pulling my father's head close to hers and kissing my forehead as though it were a final goodbye. 'I'll manage, somehow.'

My father hesitated for a moment, then took me from my mother's arms. 'Pray attend carefully to my words, Joseph,' he addressed me quite forcefully as both he and my mother hastened to remove their shoes. 'I am going to put you upon my back, and you must hold on for dear life. Do you understand?'

I nodded, tearfully, unable to speak. Terror had stolen my voice. Grabbing Mother's hand, Father climbed upon the rails and helped us up. 'It's now or never,' he declared. 'The ship is going to roll. We must be clear of her before she does, or we will be crushed beneath her.'

A large wave hit the ship as he spoke and its timbers shuddered violently. We were in the water before we knew it. It was cold. Bitterly cold.

The waves being big, and the current strong, Mother struggled to swim in her flouncy dress and didn't last very long. One minute she was there, and the next she wasn't. Father tried his best to stifle his grief, and his guilt, and to focus all of his energies on saving me. But swimming with a child on your back is difficult and all too soon he, too, was exhausted.

Father was now in a pitiful dilemma. If he tried to save me, we would both drown. But were he to let go of me, he might, even yet, be capable of saving himself. It was a decision no parent should ever have to make, and he had all but resigned himself to an honourable death when Fortune decided to smile upon us.

A wooden trunk that had broken free from the hold suddenly popped up to the left of us — a crested travelling trunk in which persons of quality would pack their belongings. Two belt straps of the finest leather crossed the lid and were buckled parallel to the latch. Rising and falling with the waves the trunk lay just an arm's length from Father. He instantly reached for it.

'Attend to my words now, Joseph,' he instructed with a calm that belied the severity of our predicament. 'I fear I cannot carry you much further, so I'm going to loosen these straps and, when I do, I want you to slip your arms through them and hold on as tightly as you have been holding on to me.'

'But I'm tired,' I cried. 'I want *you* to carry me.'

'Alas, I can no longer do so,' said Father. 'My strength is waning. I know not how long it will last. Now, whatever you do, Joseph, and however long it takes, promise me you will not let go of these straps. We ride on an incoming tide. Sooner or later it will wash this trunk ashore. Should we be separated, just you hold fast until it reaches land. Eventually, someone will discover you and return you to me. Pray child, tell me that you understand?'

Father battled bravely to stay alongside me, but the current was so strong that eventually we were forced apart. Afraid to look for fear of what horrors I might observe, I closed my eyes and hung on for dear life, weeping for the loss of my mother and the fear of what might yet happen to my father and me.

I was on the crest of a wave about a hundred yards from the beach when I saw my father scramble ashore. There were people on the beach and in my heart I believed that he was saved. But he had merely survived one ordeal to crawl headfirst into another. Those people on the beach, unfortunately, were not waiting to assist him, but to kill him.

My father was beaten lifeless by the waiting

mob, a fate that befell every other man who managed to reach the beach alive. If I had been frightened before, I was positively terrified now. I did not understand what was happening. It was against the natural order of things, and beyond my childish comprehension.

The few rowboats that had been launched from the beach offered no more in the way of assistance. Ignoring the pitiful pleas of every living soul that was in the water, they rowed instead to recover the trunks and barrels that had broken loose from the ship before they could be washed towards Rogerstown or dashed to destruction on the rocks.

The trunk to which I was strapped was but a stone's throw from the shore when a woman waded into the waves and began to bear down on me. Ignoring the scolding of the men and the catcalls of the other women who stood behind her, she dragged me and the trunk ashore. To this day I cannot tell you with any degree of certainty whether it was the sight of the trunk that first drew her into the water, or the sight of me clinging to it.

The beach was littered with dead bodies by that time. Some had simply drowned and been washed ashore; others, like my father, had been clubbed to death by the mob. Had I not been shaking from the cold, I would almost certainly have been shaking with terror, for in the very moment of my rescue I feared I was to share my father's fate.

I was four years old and terrified beyond all description. They let me live, I suppose, because I was still but a child, and perhaps also because the woman who had rescued me had retained, or would claim to have retained, at least one Christian scruple.

The light our captain had followed, as you

must surely have gathered by now, had not been from another ship, but from those heartless villains on the shore. They had deliberately hung a false light on the dunes in the hope of tempting our ship into shallow waters, where they expected it would founder and shed its cargo.

The hanging of false lights was not a common occurrence in these parts back then, even if the practice was widely spoken of elsewhere. The local people had long enjoyed a reputation as expert smugglers, but deliberate shipwrecking was something new, and not everyone who dwelled hereabouts did actively approve of it.

That having been said, there were also precious few amongst those who opposed the practice who would dare to speak publicly against it, for all were afraid of Barnaby Sherwin, the intimidating bull of a man who had organized it. All, that is, bar his wife – the woman who had rescued me.

Though her husband and son were violently against the idea, Elinor Sherwin brought me home with her that night. Her actions were also far from popular amongst her neighbours, as they flew in the face of a long observed local tradition – that the sea was entitled to her prey.

In saving a person from drowning, it was locally believed, you were cheating the sea of her prey and she would eventually take her revenge upon you for so doing by ensuring that you would eventually meet your death at the hands of the person you had saved. One way or another, it was said, the sea would have her due and it was folly to interfere.

But Mrs Sherwin had not been born in the locality and was very little influenced by local taboos. No one in *her* family, she declared to any and all who would challenge her, was going to kill a child, even if it was an English child. Surprisingly, they let her have her way. She was, after all, Barnaby Sherwin's wife. There were limits to their madness I suppose, just as there was to their courage. No one, but no one, dared to cross Barnaby Sherwin.

Despite the fact that she had taken me from the sea, Elinor Sherwin would never show any real affection for me. I would never be anything more to her than a trophy of sorts, a living reminder to be forever waved in the face of those who had participated in the taking of innocent lives. Torn between her Christian conscience and her loyalty to her husband and son, she would forever look upon me the way some people look upon a crucifix.

The Sherwins lived in a two-bedroom cottage at Turvey, about a mile and a half inland from the shore. Barnaby and his wife, Elinor, slept in one bedroom, while their twenty-year-old son, Patrick, and his wife, Betty, slept in the other. There was no bedroom for me and would not be for a very long time.

Mrs Sherwin gave me a couple of blankets and cleared a space for me on the parlour floor close to the hearth. For weeks I cowered in that corner like a whimpering pup, never saying a word to anyone and having to be coaxed out with food, which I would only accept from the hands of Mrs Sherwin.

I was alive, and I suppose I should have been grateful for that, but I wasn't. I was distraught – traumatised by all that I had seen and unable to enjoy but the odd night of peaceful slumber on account of the dreadful memories that would frequently invade my dreams and cause me to waken, screaming and crying, and covered in a film of cold sweat.

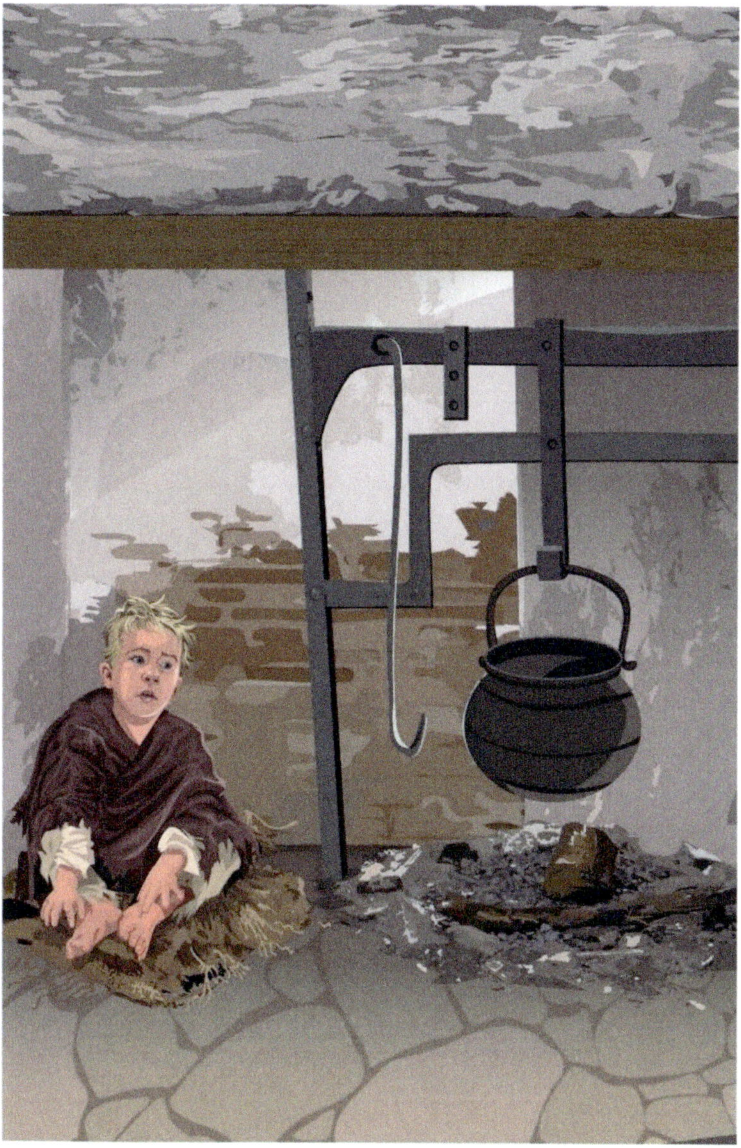

I longed for some comfort, for a pair of consoling arms to wrap themselves about me and tell me that everything would be okay, that I was safe now, that I would be loved and cared for. But it wasn't to be. Quite the opposite.

My tender years notwithstanding, I would be beaten by Barnaby for night wetting or failing to answer when spoken to. But I never cried. Whenever the urge to do so would rise in my chest, I would remember Father and Mother and push it back down.

I would not cry, I vowed constantly to myself. I would never, ever, allow Barnaby Sherwin the satisfaction, or the provocation, of one single hot tear.

Sitting in my allotted corner, and rocking myself for comfort, I tried desperately to convince myself that, by some miracle, my parents might have survived and would eventually come looking for me. But, deep down, I believe I understood that they had not, and would not. It took some time, but eventually, I came to accept that they were gone forever and to reconcile myself to my captivity. By degrees I allowed the Sherwins to take ownership of me.

'Well, now that you have it, ' said Barnaby Sherwin to his wife one day, 'what's to be done with it? All skin and bones, so it is, more like a little girl than a boy. Can't see that it's ever going to be of much use around here. If you'd wanted a pet, you might have said and I'd have got you a dog.'

'Now don't you worry about him,' Mrs Sherwin replied. 'I'll soon put colour in those cheeks and flesh on those bones. He'll prove a fine investment yet and, come Judgement Day, this woman, at least, will be able to say that she discharged her Christian duty. You mark my words, Barnaby Sherwin, as sure as there's salt in the sea, there'll be a reckoning to be paid for what happened that night. No one said anything about murder, and I would not have gone with you if I had known of such intentions.'

'Ha!' Barnaby snorted. 'Judgement day be damned! Every day is judgement day for the likes of us. Seems to me as though we were born judged. Why else would some be born rich and others be born poor? Why else would as fine and cultured a race of people as ever walked this earth be now subject to the barbarism of a foreign crown? Where's the justice in that, eh? Answer me that woman. Answer me that.'

She never did of course, for Barnaby Sherwin had an answer for everything. His answers didn't always make sense or correspond to the religious beliefs that he professed to follow, but it was useless to argue with him. Barnaby Sherwin was deaf to every opinion but his own.

Mrs Sherwin was wont to throw the words 'Christian duty' in the face of her husband with annoying regularity but, truth be told, she spent very little time on her knees, nor was any such display ever encouraged in that virtueless hovel.

Religion to Mrs Sherwin was like her best cloak, worn only on Sundays and holy days. Her one and only act of mercy had been simply a charm that she had pocketed as insurance against damnation, the fear of which rarely softened her character, or moved her to anything resembling compassion.

Her heart was as hard as the conditions she lived in, but she understood the nature of guilt, and the power it could give one person over another. And so she kept me safe, wearing me like a halo before her husband and her neighbours. My presence, in her mind at least, made her someone.

Not everyone, however, could make sense of Mrs Sherwin's motivation and, for the first few weeks of my life at Turvey, I became the talk of the peninsula. Neighbours that Elinor Sherwin hadn't seen for months would suddenly find an excuse to visit, hoping to catch a glimpse of her little foundling. There wasn't one that didn't think she was mad to keep me, but there was only one who would dare to tell her so.

A Mrs McAllister came by the cottage one day. She paused at the half-door as though thinking of coming in, but ultimately thought better of it. Leaning on the closed bottom half of the door, she absorbed the curious sight of an English child cowering in the corner of the Sherwins' parlour like an ill-treated pup.

'Taking quite the risk there, aren't you, after all that he's seen?' she queried casually without so much as an introductory greeting. 'Should have left him to the sea, so you should. You know what happens to folks who cheat the sea of her prey.'

'Just because I married into this family doesn't mean I'm going to believe every old wives' tale that comes out of their mouths,' Mrs Sherwin snapped back. 'And it wasn't the sea that preyed upon that ship now, was it? In any case, I've as much right to keep a servant as any fine squire. Sure aren't these boats that are sailing lately for the Americas crammed full of orphans like him, waiting to be sold into servitude? Well, I didn't buy him, did I? I saved his life. So as far as I'm concerned, he owes me that life, whether he likes it or not. It could so easily have been otherwise. Come judgement day, the Lord will know I did my Christian duty. Until then this one will pay his way.'

'Suit yourself,' said Mrs McAllister. 'You lot always do. But you mark my words, Elinor Sherwin, no good will come of this, no good at all.'

Mrs Sherwin shrugged her shoulders and got on with her washing. I could tell there was more she wanted to say but didn't dare to. That was the way of it in small communities. Sometimes you simply had to swallow a goodly dose of pride and anger to get along with your neighbours.

But at least Mrs McAllister had seen me in the flesh and was under no illusions about what, or who, I was. There were many, however, in those early days, who never got next nor near Mrs Sherwin's half-door and who, starved of details, began to invent their own.

One story doing the rounds was that I was

the son of a French smuggler and could not even speak the King's English. Another was that I was the son of a British lord who was being held by the Sherwins for ransom. Neither, of course, could have been further from the truth.

But if I had thought that Elinor Sherwin's brief notoriety would lead her to develop even the slightest of maternal affection for me, I was to be sadly mistaken. I would never be accepted as part of that family. I was to be their servant boy, nothing more and nothing less. My life was to be one of captivity, at least until I grew tall enough to reach the top bolt of the cottage door, a bolt that was only ever locked at night.

The first few months passed like a bad dream, but I gradually settled into the rhythm of life with the Sherwins, rising at dawn and retiring at dusk, living by the light of the sun and the light of the fire, and rarely, if ever, lighting a lantern, the irony of which will not be lost on you. Lamp oil, you see, was expensive.

I was immediately set to work, of course, and one of my earliest chores was to accompany Mrs Sherwin on her weekly walks to collect firewood. 'You can work, or you can starve,' she would threaten. 'Don't make me regret going into the sea to rescue you. We've little enough as it is to be wasting it on leeches.'

The mornings after a storm were our busiest. We would all head out to gather driftwood from the beaches or whatever bounty had fallen from the trees of the big estates. We'd have to rise very early on such days and be quick about our collection, for the landlords would charge us with theft if they caught us collecting it. Every branch and twig had its price and you took timber from the great estates or private beaches at your peril.

I was just four years of age that first year in Turvey – too small and too weak to be of much use in the field. And so Mrs Sherwin gave me menial jobs about the farm, such as fetching water, sweeping the hearth, or feeding the pig and the hens, the only living creatures that ever seemed glad to see me.

'You're spoiling him,' Barnaby would often say to her. 'He should be out labouring in the field or learning to trap, not tied to your apron strings.'

'Time enough for that,' Mrs Sherwin would answer back. 'He needs building up first.'

I had been with the Sherwins a little over a year when Patrick's wife, Betty, died following a difficult childbirth. He grieved sorely for a while, but it quickly became apparent that he was unsuited to the care of an infant and so Baby Fergus was moved to his grandparent's room, where Mrs Sherwin undertook the care of him.

May the good Lord forgive me, but I was secretly glad of Betty's death. Foolish waif that I was, I thought that I might now get to move into Patrick's room to sleep. But it wasn't to be. I was left, as befitted my station, to sleep like a hound by the hearth.

As one day followed another, and my understanding of my new life grew, I was gradually trusted to go places on my own for, strange as it might seem to someone who has never been held captive, I had come to accept my slave masters as a kind of family – a family to which I belonged, but could never be a part of. Children, they say, are resilient, and can adjust to almost any circumstance, given time. Well, I would say there is at least some truth in that, because that is more or less what happened to me.

As the years flew past, and I got bigger and stronger, I would often be sent to fetch seaweed from the shore to fertilize the potatoes. Given a sack, Barnaby would instruct me to walk the three long miles to Balcarrick Beach and to not return until the sack was full. It would take the best part of an hour to get to the shore, and about half as long again to get back.

You have no idea how heavy a sack of wet seaweed can get, or how awkward it can be to carry. And I would *have* to carry it, for there would be blue hell to pay when I got back if I had ripped the sack or scuffed it by dragging it.

One windy day I came back early. There had been a storm the night before and the high tide mark was fringed with seaweed. I hadn't had to walk very far to fill my sack. Upon my return, I relieved myself of my burden and sat down by the door to catch my breath and rest my weary arms.

Not having been expected, and my return having passed unnoticed, nobody within the cottage had any reason to modify their words or their behaviour, and, with the cottage half-door sitting partially ajar, every spoken word within could be overheard clearly without.

'We've barely got enough food to feed ourselves,' Patrick was moaning to his father, 'let alone for Mother's English pup. It's as plain as a pikestaff the little runt will never be fitted for farm work. So why don't we just rid ourselves of him now and save the cost of his keep? There are four of us as it is, counting the baby, and barely enough food to go around. It's madness I tell you. Utter madness.'

'You're not suggesting we do away with him

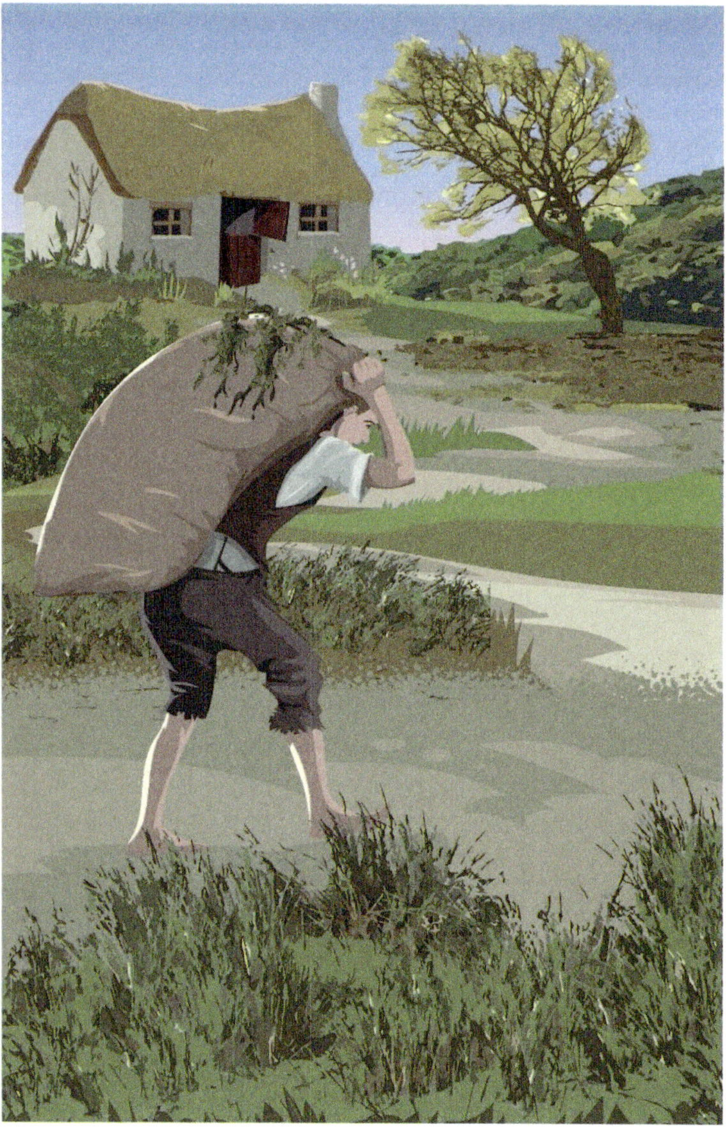

I hope,' said Barnaby. 'Your mother would never stand for it. She wears his presence like a halo and it grates on my nerves to be so frequently judged, but I know her well enough to know that her silent scolding is but the bite of a flea compared to the scald that would follow his disappearance. Would be a living hell, so it would.'

'I have no doubts about that, Father,' said Patrick, 'and though I have been sorely tempted to do away with the little runt, on more than one occasion, it was something else entirely I had in mind. What age be he now, do you think?'

'Five? Six? Hard to tell,' said Barnaby. 'Why do you ask?'

'Because, Father, in a year or so he'll most likely be too old,' said Patrick, 'for I was thinking, of late, that we might yet be able to sell him, and tell mother that he ran away.'

'Sell him?' said Barnaby. 'Pray tell, who around these parts, would want to buy *him*? He's of precious little use to us as it is?'

'Not here,' said Patrick. 'In Dublin. Children are kidnapped every day up in the city. I've seen it happen with my own eyes. There's a thriving market for indentured servants in the Americas. There's many a ship's captain offering easy money for them.'

'You don't say?' said Barnaby. 'Go on, I'm listening.'

'Even if he was to prove unsuited to that, we could still sell him to a chimney sweep. He's possibly skinny enough for that. Or perhaps one of the city gangs might take him and put him with a bowl to beg. There are so many possibilities. Just say the word and I'll take care of it. I know of a woman who'll pay five pounds for him tomorrow, no questions asked. Just think father, five pounds!'

'A tidy sum to be sure,' said Barnaby, 'and I've long been thinking it's high time we reaped some benefit from him. But I fear the pup is already too big for a sweep's boy, and as yet too young to make a decent cabin boy. Let me think about it. The idea, though it be untimely, has merit. But, in the meantime, there's a ditch that needs digging and a fence that needs mending.'

If I had failed to realise it before, I knew for certain now that in the eyes of Barnaby and Patrick Sherwin I was no different than a common beast of burden. But knowing it was one thing, knowing what to do about it, quite another.

I vowed, henceforward, that I would strive to make myself indispensable. Whatever labours they would heap upon me, whatever bruises and blisters I had to endure, however dirty or smelly the task, I would complete it without a word of complaint. I would make of myself an asset too valuable to be sold. And I would be patient. I would await my opportunity to escape, however long it took.

I had, by this time, spent almost a third of my short and unfortunate life with the Sherwins. And though there was never much affection shown towards me, I'd grown accustomed to living in Turvey, and had come to think of it as home. I no longer had a clear memory of anywhere else. Memories of our early years are so quickly lost. I know not why.

On only one occasion did I experience even the merest hint of compassion from any of them, and that was the autumn I had the misfortune to catch a fever. Barnaby, believing that I was malingering, was about to beat me for my sluggishness when Mrs Sherwin intervened.

'Look at him, Barnaby,' she shouted. 'He's

perspiring, and it's not from fear of you or your belt, I can tell you. The child has a fever.'

'Fever, is it?' said Barnaby, 'then get him out of here before we all catch it.'

And so it was that I was removed from the cottage and exiled like some noxious animal to the pigsty, just in case the fever I'd contracted should prove to be contagious. But at least I was given fresh straw, and plenty of blankets to keep me warm. Three times a day Mrs Sherwin would also bring me bread and hot soup and, before she left, would test my temperature by placing a cool hand on my forehead.

That simple touch was the closest I ever came to feeling mothered by her, and it represented a rare breach in the severity of her character. For a brief while, it instilled in me the hope that, deep down in her soul, she might have nurtured some well-concealed maternal feeling for me.

But it wasn't to be. As soon as the fever had subsided, and I was allowed to return to the house, she returned to her habitual ways. The concern she had shown for me, was no more than she would show to any ailing farm animal.

As the years flew by, the memories of my early childhood slowly faded. But even if I had managed to retain them, it was not as if I could suddenly run back to Liverpool was it? I mean, how could I possibly escape at just eight years of age? How was I to know whom I could trust? Even the local constables appeared to be friendly with Barnaby Sherwin, for they seemed only too willing to turn a blind eye to his activities.

I was trapped. Well and truly trapped. For better, or for worse, this was my life now. I was just another cock in a cage. I had no choice but to make the best of it.

There was never any suggestion of book learning at the Sherwin's. Like most poor families, there was always far too much to be done, and chores never failed to multiply to meet the number of hands that were available to do them. And so I never learnt to read or write, and neither did anyone else in that accursed household.

Not a single book or newspaper did I ever see in all my time there, not even a Bible. My parents had been educated people and had often read to me from the Good Book. And so, even at that tender age, I knew enough to worry about my future.

I was learning nothing about the world, and gaining no skills that I could trade for a living wage other than that of a common labourer. I knew not what was to become of me. But I was a bright child. I understood enough to know that it would not be good.

At the age of ten, I was finally set to work alongside Barnaby Sherwin in the fields. I dreaded every single back-breaking day of it. If ever I struggled physically or delayed in obeying his commands, he'd lash out at me with his tongue or, just as frequently, with his hands.

Barnaby was forever tormenting me. It mattered little what I was doing at the time, or how well I was doing it. If the mood overtook him, he would lash out at me. Half the time I never saw it coming or had any inkling of the reason. Sometimes, even if he hadn't been around all day, he'd come looking for me, just to have someone to swing at. He broke my nose one time. It never straightened properly.

Complaining to Mrs Sherwin was useless. 'You must have done something to warrant it,' was all she'd ever say. 'Spare the rod and spoil the child.'

Such was Barnaby's temper and his relationship with the bottle that I had long since learned to sleep with my head in the corner, my back to the wall, and my knees tucked up to my chest. In this position, a swinging boot would catch only the back of my legs. They would bruise and ache, but it was preferable to allowing Barnaby's boot to catch a bone.

I often promised myself that someday I would get even. I vowed it almost as frequently as I promised myself that, one day, I would find a way to escape. But these were but empty promises, for the reality of escape had not been fully considered.

Before you judge me harshly for my complacency, I beg of you to consider the following. If I did flee from the Sherwin's, what exactly would I be escaping to? Would it be any better than where I was? You might well have done different, but you cannot underestimate the fear of the unknown on a child. Indeed, I believe it was *that* more than the fear of being caught and punished that kept me so long a willing captive of these brutes. Better the devil you know, I would think to myself, than the devil you don't.

Barnaby's increasingly dark moods sprang primarily from the absence of his only son, Patrick, who by now had grown up and taken residence with a widow from Coldwinters. Barnaby would bear the absence of his son with little grace and contrive to blame me for having driven him away. In truth, I had little to do with it, other than having for a long time been a cause of dispute between them.

It was, to be sure, a strange state of affairs, for Patrick's widow woman was much older than he, and somewhat past the age of forty. But, despite her age, it was widely reported, she did not want for beauty and her great accumulation of years was mitigated by the fact that she was a woman of large fortune and far from miserly in the sharing of it.

And yet, though Patrick now had real money in his pockets, Barnaby and Elinor Sherwin never saw a shilling of it. And though they could well have done with some of that silver occasionally, they were always too proud to ask and it never once occurred to Patrick to offer. In his eyes, one might suppose, it wasn't his money to give. But that would be to credit the rogue with scruples.

Patrick and his widow woman lived together as man and wife but, being at that carefree stage of life, the lady in question never once entertained the notion of marrying him. And neither did she ever show any willingness to allow herself to be put in a situation where she would have to relinquish control of her fortune, or, for that matter, to raise another man's child. Selfish rogue that he was, that suited Patrick just fine.

It was left, therefore, to Barnaby and Elinor to raise Patrick's son, Fergus, who was by then about six. He had been given Patrick's bedroom after it became apparent that Patrick would not be returning, and I had been allowed to share with him.

Finally, I had a bed, even if it had to be shared and, though we were not related in any way, for a short time I came to think of Fergus as a younger brother. We would work side by side and even play around together when Barnaby wasn't about, in the way, I imagine, most brothers do.

We became quite the team, Fergus and I. Mrs Sherwin was getting old and was happy enough to make it our exclusive job to collect driftwood and, more latterly, coal. Whenever the coal boats came in, Fergus and I would hike over to the harbour at Newport with a wicker basket and scavenge for any loose nuggets that had fallen onto the quay or into the water during unloading.

If we were lucky, we might bring back half a basket a week. It wasn't a lot but, over the course of a year, we might gather enough to give us a week or two of coal fires during the winter. Unlike the timber in the woodpile, the coal would be preserved for the coldest winter nights, when the extra heat was desperately needed, and greatly appreciated.

Every now and again, Patrick would come back to Turvey his dress and manner so much altered as to make him scarcely recognisable. He came, most times, to see his son, Fergus; at others to assist his father in that trade that no one would ever dare to speak of in my presence.

Patrick and Barnaby would often disappear of a night on some secret business I suspected was far from honest labour, and they would rarely return before dawn. Not once was I ever invited to accompany them, and so secretive were they in their endeavours that it took me years to fathom the nature of their activities.

I remember clearly the day the penny dropped. I was walking with Mrs Sherwin through the village of Donabate when I heard a small handbell ringing in the distance. I wasn't the only one to have heard it, though I was, perhaps, the only local person to have fancied it signalled the approach of a leper, or some other unfortunate soul rendered unclean by disease.

'Turn around,' said Mrs Sherwin urgently, 'and face the wall.'

'What for?' I asked. 'What have I done now?'

'Just do as you are told,' she said. 'A body can't tell what a body don't see.'

I did as I was bid. But, hearing a horse and cart passing behind me, I attempted to sneak a quick peek. But I had scarcely begun to turn my head when Mrs Sherwin gave me such a clip around the ear that it was still smarting an hour later.

It was never expressly said, but I eventually deduced that the entire community was involved in the smuggling trade and that, whenever the smugglers wanted to cart their contraband through the village, a handbell would be rung to warn the villagers to turn their faces to the wall.

By this simple trick, none could identify the smugglers and none would be telling a lie, or committing a sin, should they later be asked by a local magistrate to swear on the Holy

Bible that they had not seen anything or recognised anyone.

The smuggled goods were almost always sold, but occasionally Barnaby would keep something back for himself so that he and Mrs Sherwin could, as he would put it, 'live like royalty for a night'.

Mostly it would be sugar loaves and the occasional bottle of brandy. But, every now and again, Barnaby would bring home something luxurious, something really precious, like tea. One particular night he came home with a small brown bag and plonked it triumphantly on the parlour table.

'Now then, Elinor me darling,' he trumpeted, 'put the kettle on the fire and bring out the best cups.'

'What is it you've got now,' she asked. 'More tea is it? Was there not a drop of brandy or port to be had this dark night?'

'Ne'er a bit of it,' said Barnaby, 'and tea it is to be sure. But this is no common or garden green tea, mind you, this here is *bohea*, the most expensive tea in all the world. A black tea, all the way from China. So get that kettle on, Mrs Sherwin, for tonight you'll sup like a queen.'

I never got to taste tea, be it cheap green or expensive black, but from the way Mrs Sherwin would squint when she drank it, I guessed it to be a bitter drink. I do not believe she was overly fond of it, nor do I expect I would have been either.

But Elinor Sherwin had a weakness for extravagant gestures and would never disappoint her husband by saying she didn't appreciate them. After all, it was the closest she ever got to receiving a gift from him and, if only for one night and such trophies made her beloved husband feel as if he was someone important, then she would act her cotton socks off.

On such occasions, I would also be reminded, if ever I needed reminding, that no matter what punishments Barnaby Sherwin would ever inflict upon me, I would never receive any comfort or compassion from his wife. They might have had their disagreements, but they were very much a team, each as responsible as the other for the hardships I endured.

It was about a dozen years since I was pulled from the surf by Mrs Sherwin when I first encountered 'the two Johns'. John Ryan and John Farrell were cousins who lived together in the Ryans' cottage in The Burrow of Portrane.

John Ryan was a youth of five and ten years back then, and John Farrell an orphaned cousin of six and ten who had been taken in by the Ryans. Everyone knew them as 'the two Johns' because you rarely saw one without the other. We met after mass one Sunday morning – the only day that we didn't have to work – and fell to chatting.

The two Johns had a small sailboat and were excellent sailors. They invited me to come fishing with them, an activity that was to become one of the few joys of my miserable youth. From that day forward, the cousins and I would take the boat out and go fishing after Sunday mass, for as long as the summer lasted. The Sherwins rarely allowed me free time, but they always made an exception for this, they being very partial to a bit of fresh mackerel.

We did not have rods or nets or any such thing, just makeshift lines and hooks. We would just drop our lines over the edge, sit together in silence, and wait. Little in the way of conversation ever passed between us while the lines were in the water. But that never made us feel uncomfortable. Indeed, it often felt, in those quiet moments, that we shared more than could ever have been shared with words.

You see, we understood the misery of each other's lives. We knew what we were escaping from, however briefly, and we knew what each of us would have to return to when the fishing was done. We appreciated the value of a few moments of peace and quiet, and not one among us was ever in haste to spoil it.

It was mainly mackerel that we caught and, if we were lucky enough to catch one, we often caught many, for we always used the first catch of the day as bait, and there was no better bait for mackerel than mackerel itself. In the beginning, I would borrow an old line that had once belonged to John Farrell's father, But then one day he surprised me by telling me I could keep it.

'A gift,' he said.

I almost cried with gratitude. It had been so long since anyone had shown me such kindness that I had all but forgotten how it felt. But I didn't cry. I never cried. Perhaps things might have gone better for me if I had, for emotion, as I have learned to my cost, can never truly be constrained.

The two Johns were competent sailors and strong rowers, and they knew the waters and currents of the Fingal coast almost as well as they knew the roads. Mostly we fished off Portrane, but occasionally, during the height of summer, we would venture further afield.

In late May or early June, for instance, if the tides were favourable, we would often sail over to Lambay Island to watch the puffins pushing the rabbits from their burrows. If the waters

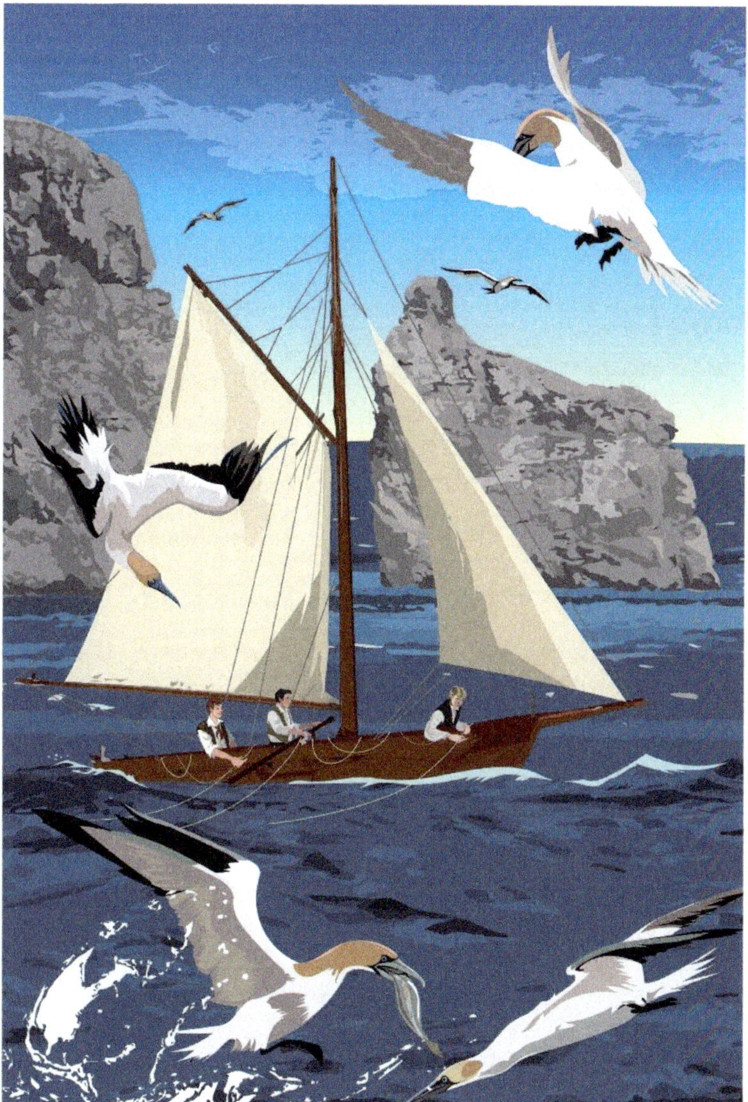

were calm and we had a fair wind, we might even venture as far as Ireland's Eye to watch the gannets diving for fish.

I believe that this was my favourite sight in all the world. Gannets are impressive birds and watching them dive was about as exciting a thing as my young eyes would ever get to see. I envied them their freedom and the thrill of the dive.

Occasionally, if we happened to arrive at Ireland's Eye during the last week of June, or the first week of July, we would anchor the boat off the west beach, stow the oars, and wade ashore. It was a small island and, unlike Lambay, was uninhabited. For a few precious hours we could pretend that it was ours, and ours alone.

Our favourite pastime was to climb the hill to see the seagull hatchlings. There would be two or three in each nest, and they were the most adorable of all the chicks that would be born each summer. You daren't get too close, however, for the mother gull would attack you if you did.

Some days, when we'd had a good catch, we would haul in our lines early and take a half dozen or so fish ashore and cook them over an open fire at the ruined church with the stump of a circular tower at one end. Only we never called it a church. That would have felt too much like sacrilege. We called it 'the den'.

Sometimes we'd play at being Vikings and have sword fights with pieces of driftwood. We'd play at raiding the den, pretending to carry off gold and imagining all the things we would do if we ever did find some buried treasure.

But then, all too soon, it would be over, and we'd have to return to our hopelessly dismal lives. The only treasure we ever took from that island was hope – a reason to survive until the following week, or the following summer.

By the time I'd reached my fourteenth year, Barnaby Sherwin was an old man and most of the physical farm work was being done by myself and Fergus. We laboured well together for a time, but the day Fergus finally learnt of my origins, everything changed and, by the time he had reached his nineteenth year, he was treating me no better than Barnaby.

I should have departed then, I was certainly old enough to have done so, but I lacked the confidence and had become habituated to my condition.

By that time I had also, coincidentally, begun to see less and less of the two Juliuses. The beginnings of that particular estrangement had its roots, I do believe, in a certain Sunday afternoon on Portrane Beach. We were out digging for lugworm at low tide when I spotted the remains of what appeared to be a small shark washed up on the tide ribbed sand.

'Hey John,' I called absently. 'Come and look at this.'

They both stopped digging, unsure of which of them was being called.

I laughed.

'Don't you ever get tired of having the same name?' I asked.

'Only when people laugh,' shouted John Ryan.

'He's messing with you,' said John Farrell, as he approached me. 'And you speak true, Joseph Daw, having the same Christian name can be a bother at times. But I suppose it does help to remind people that we are family. We were both named after our grandfather, you see. My mother was Slugger's sister. That's why the Ryans took me in, blood being thicker than water and all that.'

'Slugger' was John Ryan's father. A fisherman who worked out of Rogerstown, when he was sober enough to turn up for work. His real name was William Ryan, but everyone called him 'Slugger' on account of his violent temper and his reputation as a bar-room brawler.

Slugger was lightning-quick to take offence, and just as quick to swing his fists. His poor wife could testify to that, not that she ever would. But the truth of the matter was too often broadcast upon her face and arms. There was only so much you could conceal in a small tightly-knit community.

'Both your parents are dead then,' I said, trying to sound sympathetic and remove the suspicion that I might have been making fun of my companions.

'Caught the bloody flux,' said John Farrell, lowering his voice. 'I was four. Had nowhere else to go, so Slugger took me in. There are times, almost every day to be honest, when I wish that he hadn't.'

'At least he's family,' I countered. 'My parents were lost in a storm and the Sherwins rescued me and took me in. But they're not family, and have never treated me as such.'

John Farrell's eyebrows raised momentarily, as though surprised by my ignorance. In hindsight, I have come to believe that, even then, he knew far more of my story than I did. That brief and private conversation, however, made me feel connected to him, if only for having lost my parents at the same age as he had lost his.

Of the two Johns, John Farrell was always the quieter of the two and, for a while, I mistook his quiet manner for gentleness. Alas, he would prove to be no less brutal, or mercenary, than his cousin, John Ryan, the dominant personality of our little band. Ryan had firm opinions on everything and always liked to feel as if he was in charge.

'What you got here then?' he asked, as he finally condescended to join us.

'Looks like a baby shark,' I replied.

He flipped it over with his boot.

'That's no shark,' he said. 'It's just a dogfish. Let's see what she's been eating.'

Taking from his pocket a small bone-handled knife he proceeded to slit open the belly of the fish.

'Well, would you look at that,' he said, sticking the knife into the sand as he separated the two sides of the fish's belly with his hands. 'Shrimp!'

I said nothing, for I had recognised the knife. It was Barnaby Sherwin's. His initials were burned into the handle.

'Where did you get that?' I asked.

'Found it,' snapped John Ryan. 'You saying I didn't?'

He spoke so aggressively that I knew better than to challenge him, for as the twig is bent, so is the tree inclined, and John Ryan was becoming as quick to take offence as his notorious father.

Some weeks later, while we were out fishing off Lambay, the same youth took from his pocket a silver hip flask and offered me a sip.

'No thanks,' I said. 'I'm not partial to whiskey.'

'Go on,' said John Farrell. 'It's good stuff. Try it. You'll like it.'

'No thanks,' I said. 'I'd rather not.'

'Becoming a regular little saint aren't you,' said John Ryan. 'Be too good for the likes of us soon, I'm thinking.'

'Priesthood next, is what *I'm* thinking,' laughed John Farrell.

I could do little but laugh with them, but I could see that they were changing; that we were drifting apart. It wasn't just the whiskey that informed me, it was the silver hip flask, for I knew that neither of them could have come honestly by so precious a thing. It simply had to have been stolen, just like Barnaby Sherwin's knife.

With the two Johns drifting by degrees into petty crime, it came as little surprise to anyone that summer, to hear that they had signed on with a smuggler captain from Rush. He kept them busy, sailing back and forth to the Isle of Man. I didn't know it at the time, but we would never fish together again.

Had circumstances been different I might well have joined them, for I valued their friendship and was loath to lose it. But I had never entirely lost my Liverpool accent and there was not a living soul for miles around that did not know my story. I was seen, not as a fellow creature, but as something base and untrustworthy – an outsider.

By this time I had also begun to be offered occasional labour on the Archbishop's farm at Newbridge House. It was backbreaking work, but pleasurable in its way, in that it allowed me to set my hands to an honest purpose that did not involve labouring alongside the foul tongue and swinging fists of Barnaby Sherwin.

Alas, I never saw a shilling of my wage. Being still but a boy, they were given to Barnaby. I hadn't the courage, or self-confidence, to argue otherwise.

The only gift I had in my favour was a pleasing appearance, for I was a fair and handsome youth. And yet, there was not a girl in the locality who would afford me a second glance, purely on account of my being an 'outsider'. Most of the time I would timidly suffer the shunning of my person, but occasionally, something approaching pride would rise within me and I would feel the need to puff out my chest and stand tall.

'Good morning, Mrs Hand; fine day, Mrs McAllister; nice stretch in the evenings, Mrs Smyth,' I would shout to the women as they collected water from the well, only for them to look at me sideways, as though the very act of hailing of them represented some brazen and unforgivable insolence. Not once did any of them ever return a greeting.

I've often heard it said that, in isolated communities, a reputation gained in the cradle can follow a man to his grave. Well, that was the way of it with me. I had lived all but four years of my life in Turvey and was very much part of the fabric of the peninsula. But, even still, I could never be more than a foundling to these people and I would never be considered a local.

Some reputations, however, are more justly earned than others, and the two Johns were quickly earning one as thieves. Strange as it might seem, I believe they rather enjoyed this sinister turn of events. A bad reputation, after all, was still a reputation, and far more acknowledgement than they ever got at home.

I, at least, had some vague memories of loving parents, and of a life that I could never enough remember. But the two Johns had never had much opportunity to feel loved, or to feel good about themselves, and their expectations were never high to begin with. Nobody, however, least of all myself, expected them to fall quite so low for since they joined the crew of a smuggling vessel, the two Johns had taken to drinking hard and, these days, were more often drunk than not, a fact that appeared to matter little to the captains who would employ them.

At least once a week they would sail to the Isle of Man to collect contraband and smuggle it into Rogerstown or Rush. But the little silver they would earn from this illegal trade was barely enough to feed and clothe them. It was a hard life, and it was about to get even harder.

The years passed and times changed. The British took over the Isle of Man and put a stop to the smuggling, forcing the smugglers to alter their former ways. For want of alternative employment, many inevitably drifted into privateering.

Now I've never been one to distinguish between privateering and piracy. Just because a privateer is employed by some king or other to plunder the ships of his enemy, it does not make him any less of a brigand than the rogue who raids a ship for profit. Both trades employ the use of violence, and it was the practice of violence that was to change the two Johns.

In no time at all, my old fishing companions had become the type of men who carried knives and who were not afraid to use them. Indeed, their personalities were so fundamentally altered by the experience, that I hardly knew them anymore.

And so, between the cooling of my relationship with Fergus, and my seeing less and less of the two Johns, I began to feel isolated and lonely up in Turvey. And it was that loneliness more than anything else, that finally prompted me to leave. I was, after all, no longer a child. There was nothing keeping me there but habit. And yet, without a single farthing to my name, nor any trade but that of a common labourer to rely upon, I could see little prospect for advancement in any place but the Americas.

I had no sooner decided to try my fortune in

the New World, however, than I chanced to witness a gathering that changed everything – a gathering I wish I had never had the misfortune to witness, for it was, ultimately, to prove my ruination.

Being abroad on the salt marshes that fateful afternoon, where I had been strolling in silent contemplation of my imminent departure, I chanced to return by way of Turvey Woods. Here, quite unexpectedly, I came upon a gathering in a small clearing.

It was Barnaby and Patrick Sherwin, and they were engrossed in teaching Fergus and the two Johns how to act as 'stalking horses' – the name that was at that time given to shipwreckers who walked the shore or cliffs raising and lowering a large lantern in imitation of a walking horse or the stern lantern of a ship at sea.

By means of this vile deception, they hoped

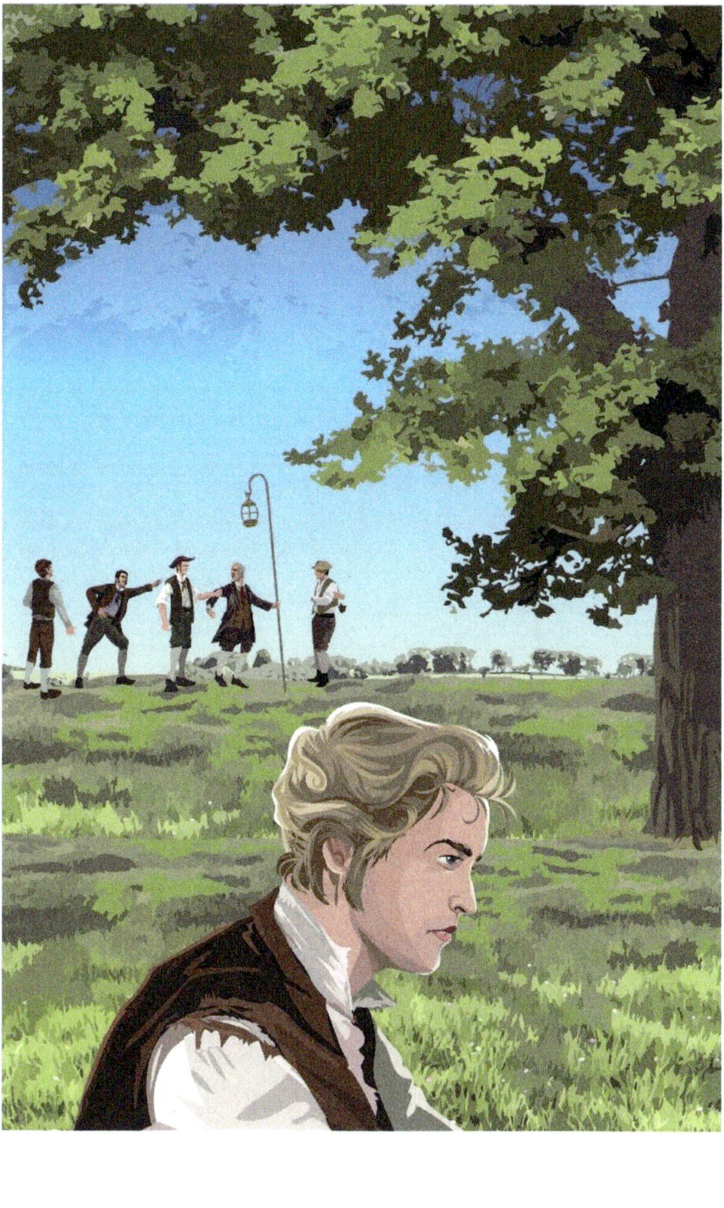

to lure a distressed ship in foul or foggy weather to its destruction. Any cargo that could then be salvaged would subsequently be taken to the nearest village to be hidden and then later sold.

The two Johns were out of work. The privateering vessel they had most recently served on was being refitted and, with no other means of making an honest shilling, they had thrown in their lot with Barnaby Sherwin. Observing me advancing upon them, Barnaby passed some muffled remark that set the entire company to laughing.

That harsh and mocking laugh wounded me more sorely than I can ever truly explain, for even yet I considered the two Johns to be my friends. To see the formerly quiet and gentle John Farrell joining so enthusiastically in the mockery of me, however, was especially wounding, for I had long believed us to have a close connection. Alas, he turned out to be not so very different from his unpredictable cousin.

This was the first I'd ever seen of the lantern the two Johns were carrying, but it took little wit on my part to recognise the mischief for which it was intended. Come a foggy night, I feared, they would be out on the cliffs with the Sherwins, intent upon a wrecking.

Sometimes, when memories are too painful, the mind practices the deceit of burying them so deep inside a man's head that they can no longer hurt him. But the body is not infallible and, sometimes, all it takes to release a buried memory is the right trigger.

Well for me, seeing that lantern was all it took to bring visions of my parents' deaths flooding to the forefront of my senses in a series of vivid flashbacks. I saw Mother in her flouncy dress fighting to stay afloat before surrendering to the inevitable and sinking forever under a wave. I saw heaps of bloodied bodies lying lifeless on the beach like so many beached dolphins, amongst them the corpse of my own father.

Most painful of all, however, was having to relive the moment when Mother was forced to choose between saving herself or saving me. As I felt again the coolness of her lips as she planted that final kiss upon my forehead, anger rose within me like a volcano. And, by God, how could it have been otherwise?

Whatever look happened to pass over my face at that precise moment, was immediately recognized by Fergus and met with another that simply burned with malice. In that instant, I knew that he suspected I intended to betray them. Fearful of initiating a chase, I walked slowly on, skirting the edge of the clearing, pretending indifference, knowing full well that to run would prove too great a provocation.

Partly out of a concern for those who might yet lose their lives, and partly out of my awful thirst for vengeance, I made up my mind to act. For I was, in that brutal moment of remembrance, consumed with a terrible rage. And not your average shout and stomp kind of rage, mind you, but the kind of all-enveloping red mist that can rob even the most reasonable of men of their senses.

You do not need to know the horrible details, but that evening I destroyed that cursed lantern and I killed the Sherwins – every last accursed one of them. I killed them for all those lives that had been lost, and for all those that were soon to be lost. But mostly I killed them for the memory of every hurtful comment and act of physical cruelty that I had ever suffered at their hands, or at their bidding.

After the terrible deed was done, I sat down

in the awful stillness of that late afternoon and, for the first time in a long time, I wept. I must have cried for over an hour, before finally pulling myself together and taking what little valuables I could find about the cabin and running to the Ryans' cabin, where I concealed them in the pig-sty.

Then, and only then, did I run to a neighbour's cabin for help, all the while pretending that I had only just that moment returned from a walk and come upon the gruesome scene.

When the constables arrived, I told them that I had witnessed two men running away and that they had looked vaguely like the two Johns. Knowing that I had once been friends with the pair, and would not implicate them lightly, the constables immediately went in search of them. Unaware that they were being sought, the two Johns were easily found, arrested, and charged.

As expected, the constables, in searching the Ryans' property, discovered the valuables I had concealed within their pigsty, and a knife with Barnaby Sherwin's initials on it was found in John Ryan's pocket. That'll teach them to mock me, I thought to myself and, for a while, I felt somewhat proud of my cleverness. It was not to last.

I had committed the worst of all crimes and the worst of all betrayals. And I might have gotten away with it too, had not something quite unforeseen happened. As the bodies were being taken away, Fergus groaned. He was alive yet, but only just.

They took him to the hospital at Inns Quay, leaving me on the horns of a dilemma. If I ran away now, it would be as good as admitting my guilt, and they would surely come after me. If I stayed, it would appear as if I had nothing to hide, but then I would be relying on the fact of Fergus dying before he could talk.

Upon the toss of a coin I decided to stay put, and it proved to be the worst decision of my life. For while Fergus did indeed die shortly afterwards from his wounds, it was not before he had regained enough of his senses to identify me as the killer.

So there I was, a couple of days later, standing in the vegetable garden digging some carrots for my supper, when the landlord, Mr Birch, arrived with some constables. They took me directly to Newgate Prison, where I was questioned for hours. I persisted with my invented story but, by and large, I was not believed.

'That's not what young Fergus told us,' the constable who was questioning me would say.

'Then he must have been delirious,' I would counter. 'For what reason would I, a poor foundling, have to kill a family that has been nothing but the soul of kindness to me. Indeed, I know not what I should do now without them.'

My explanations were not entirely implausible, and it appeared as if the police were happy enough to accept them, for they were inherently lazy and could find no discernible motive on my part. Indeed the only evidence they had against me, was Fergus' testimony, which made little sense without a believable motive. On the other hand, they had more than enough evidence against the two Johns.

I had an unexpected visit, shortly after the constables had finished with me, from the prison chaplain. He had come directly from John Farrell's prison cell. He had been convinced of their innocence.

But even then, with the reverend father

prompting me to confess, I persisted with my claim of innocence. After all, I had never said that it *was* the two Johns who had committed the murders, or even that it had been them I had seen running away. I had merely said that the two figures I had seen had *looked* like them.

After the priest had left, however, I found myself recalling those days when I would go fishing with the two Johns and we would play at Vikings on Ireland's Eye. They had befriended me when no one else would, and had shared with me some of the happiest moments of my miserable youth.

A tide of guilt began, at length, to wash over me and, in the end, I found that I could no longer persist in the fraud. I could not allow those young men to hang for my sins. And so I called again for the priest, and finally made my confession. He sat with me then, a consoling hand resting permanently upon my shoulder, as I repeated the confession to the guards.

I confessed to the murders, but I never told another living soul *why* I had killed the Sherwins. I never mentioned the lamp, or the fact that the two Johns were being trained as stalking horses. My anger had cooled by then, and I no longer had the heart to land the two Johns in any more trouble than I'd already caused them. They were released the following day.

Given time to reflect, I could scarcely believe what I had done. I was utterly ashamed and horrified by it. But I could not deny it. Indeed the memory of it was a source of such constant torture to me, that I had little difficulty in resigning myself to my fate. It would, I believed, come as something of a blessed relief. I wanted it, *all* of it, to be over, and over quickly.

The worst, however, was yet to come, for one of the prison guards informed me the following morning, that the murders had, in fact, been unnecessary. Indeed, just a week or so before I committed that unspeakable crime, a young woman from Newport had gone to the magistrate in Swords and betrayed the Sherwins.

The authorities, he said, had already known about Barnaby Sherwin's intention to wreck another ship, and would have been waiting for the wreckers the next night they went out. They would, he claimed, have been caught without my interference. No lives would have been lost, and I would not have been sentenced to hang. But the deed was done. There was no going back. All I could do was pray for forgiveness.

My trial turned out to be a mercifully short affair and I was sentenced to be taken back to

95

Turvey and hung in irons. The two Johns were present for the verdict, but I could not bring myself to meet their eyes. I doubt they had any sympathy for me. I doubt anyone had.

Barbaric! That was the word the judge employed to describe my actions on that fateful night in Turvey, and that was the word the newspapers most commonly quoted in their reports. I cannot, in all honesty, argue with them, for I *had* behaved abominably *and* like a frenzied barbarian.

The following day I was brought to this very bridge here in Donabate, sealed in this gibbet and hung from this very tree. They didn't even bother to construct a gallows. A noose and a cart was all the expenditure that went into my execution, apart from the five guineas the hangman had demanded on account of his having to travel so far from the city to perform his macabre duty. Six months they left me hanging here. Six months! Now how barbaric, pray tell, was that?

You might well have heard some of the older people hereabouts using the expression 'hung as high as a Daw'. Well, now you know. That Daw was me. So, let that be a lesson to you, Master Billy. Revenge is a poison. You might have good cause to thirst for it, but you drink it at your peril.

Yonder bridge was called after me on account of the hanging. Nobody was seeking to celebrate my life, or even my death for that matter. It was just a handy way of referring to a nameless bridge. But it's something, I suppose. I mean, it's not as if I ever got a headstone, is it? And being rendered infamous for eternity is, I suppose, at least some form of remembrance.

Anyway, as I was saying, a few months after the hanging, a priest of the Roman Catholic religion happened to be passing on the Newry to Dublin stagecoach and saw my body hanging in this here gibbet. Being so far outside Dublin, it had long since been forgotten about, and nobody in these parts was willing to touch the gibbet because to do so was a criminal offence.

This passing priest, kind-hearted soul that he was, had the driver stop the coach and called on some local farmhands to come forth and help him cut me down. Well, the fellows cut me down alright, and they buried me, or rather half-buried me in this spot, gibbet and all.

The priest, by this time, had resumed his journey, the coachman being anxious to keep to his busy schedule. But no prayers were ever said over me and the grave was never properly blessed. And that, Master Billy, is why I remain here, a castaway spirit, stranded between this world and the next, longing only for eternal rest.

The farm boys that cut me down, being Turvey youths and very much afraid of ghosts, buried me on the Lusk side of the stream, it being well known that ghosts cannot cross water. This particular stretch of ground, however, is very flat and prone to flooding. Over the years the stream has changed course more than once.

It was one of these course changes that caused the bank on the Lusk side of the stream to be slowly eroded. And as the bank began to collapse, a piece of my gibbet slowly became exposed. That was not twelve months ago, I do believe. It was discovered by a local ploughboy. He took me for a Viking warrior of all things. Imagine that! After all these years I was playing at being a Viking again.

Of course the illusion was not to last. All

manner of experts were called in to excavate the gibbet and take it to some museum or other. As for my bones, they were taken to some university or other, I know not which. And so, my resting place having been defiled, my soul now remains stuck here, unable to rejoin my blessed and beloved parents on the other side.

So that, in a nutshell, Master Billy, is what I am after in the haunting of this bridge; to have someone track down my bones and give me a decent burial on consecrated ground. And, of course, I want people to finally know my side of the story. Is that too much to ask?

Look here, young sir, I own I deserved my punishment – I can scarcely pretend otherwise – but did I really deserve this? There's been far worse than me that have been allowed to move on and, if I may be allowed to say so, many of the worst of them have worn Roman collars.

My only desire is that the same mercy should be granted to me.

All I am seeking, Master Billy, is just one priest who will lend a sympathetic ear to my cause, who will grant me the mercy of a proper burial, who will accept that I was never moved by any other intention than the saving of innocent lives.

All I desire, sir, is that just one solitary priest will believe me when I say that I simply wasn't in my right mind at the time and, because my repentance is genuine and heartfelt, will grant me the mercy of absolution.

Four people died that awful night, Master Billy, and maybe they deserved to, on account of the dreadful mischief that they were planning. But I realise it was not my decision to make, or even my justice to deliver, despite all that had been done to me.

I swear by Almighty God, Master Billy, that I genuinely believed more lives would be saved by my actions than would be lost. That has to stand for something. Doesn't it?

A GUILTY CONSCIENCE

WELL NOW, THERE you have it. That was Joseph Daw's story, and more or less as he told it to me. And now, if you don't mind, I'd like you to hear mine. For if poor old Joseph was burdened with a guilty conscience, then I guess I was too. I suppose that is part of the reason why I'm telling you this story; because I made a promise I never kept.

When I got home from Daw's Bridge that first evening, my mother was laying the table for supper. My father was still in a bit of a mood about Trotsky and all manner of other stuff, and so my mother, anxious not to draw attention to my late arrival, directed me to go to my room and change out of my school uniform before supper. I was sitting on my bed when she popped her head around the bedroom door.

'Is everything okay?' she asked.

'Fine,' I said. 'Why?'

'Oh, I don't know,' she replied. 'It's just that you look a little, well, stressed. Is something worrying you? Everything okay at school?'

'Everything's fine,' I said.

What else could I do? To raise the subject of Joseph Daw, I would have had to admit where I'd been and, given the foul mood that Dad was in, that would have been like tossing a firework onto the embers of a bonfire. I suppose I was also afraid that no one would believe me, as most people still believed that ghosts only appeared at night.

Over the course of the following day, I would replay my spooky encounter over and over in my head, hoping to find some evidence of my having fallen asleep, or having tripped and knocked myself unconscious. I was desperate, you see, to find something that would enable me to chalk it all up to an hallucination, or a dream.

But I couldn't. Joseph Daw had seemed as real to me then as he does now, as solid as the ground I was standing on when he first called out to me. Despite my best efforts, he refused to be written off as a figment of my imagination.

Over the following week I asked several people about Daw's bridge and how it got its name, but everyone I asked, both teachers and neighbours alike, had a different story to tell. There was just one constant that joined the stories together, and that was the portrayal of Daw as a notorious and cold-blooded killer, a man deserving of neither mercy nor pity.

The more I asked about Daw, the more my opinion of him began to change. Maybe I was too trusting of the stories I'd been told by adults, or maybe I was still looking for an excuse to do nothing but, for the longest time, I never told another living soul about what had happened to me that day at Daw's Bridge.

I had begun to doubt myself, you see. But my doubts weren't *only* because of the stories that people were telling me about Joseph Daw, it was also because of the tree. Yes, you read that correctly. The tree!

You see, over the months that followed, I would occasionally cross Daw's Bridge with my parents whenever we caught the bus to Skerries. Each and every time we did, I couldn't help but steal a furtive glance in the direction of the leafless tree where I'd met my ghostly acquaintance.

He was never there, of course, which didn't surprise me. I never expected that he would. But then again, neither was the tree that he'd been hanging from. And that did.

Now, when have you ever heard of anything like that? A ghost tree! That was a new one on me, as I'm sure it is on you. And it was that, more than anything, that had me questioning myself. But the fact remained that I had made a promise and, as hard as I tried to forget about it, I simply couldn't.

It took a couple of years before I was finally able to pluck up the courage to do something about it. It was a summer's day in 1936, and I was dossing about the house, enjoying the school holidays. My mother, anxious to get me out from under her feet, sent me to confession, for no other reason than I hadn't been for months.

I hated going to confession. I could never think of anything to say. Even when I could, I was always too embarrassed to tell the priest. But that particular day was different. Seeing as I was going anyway, and didn't have to dig too deep to take that first step, I decided to finally fulfil the promise I'd made to Joseph Daw and tell his story to a priest.

Now, it so happened that there was a new priest in the parish that year. He was quite popular and trendy and, as luck would have it, on confession duty that very morning. I had every reason to believe that he'd be sympathetic to my dilemma. But I was wrong. So very wrong!

I sat in the pew and waited until the last of the old ladies had been and gone, before finally entering the confession box.

'Bless me, Father for I have sinned,' I

prattled nervously. 'It has been three months since my last confession… but that's not why I'm here. I'm here because I made a promise to a man to tell something to a priest, and I never did, and it's been bothering me for years.'

'I understand,' said the priest. 'A broken promise can weigh as heavily upon the soul as any other sin, but I'm sure you had your reasons, and you're here now, aren't you? Go on my child, I'm listening.'

I can't tell you how nervous I was, and how much I wanted to have the unpleasant business over and done with. But, between one thing and another, I'm afraid I didn't do poor Joseph's story justice.

'Well, father,' says I in a breathless rush, 'this man, he lived up in Turvey and he killed four people and he didn't mean to and he was sorry and they hanged him and they put his body in a cage and a priest cut him down and they buried him and it wasn't a proper burial and now he wants one and he asked me to tell the priest... and his name was Joseph Daw.'

'Well now,' said the priest. 'If that isn't a story and a half. A dare was it? Your friends waiting outside to see what I'll do? Did you think I don't read the papers too? Run along now and don't be wasting my time. You can tell your friends whatever you want but, the next time you come to confession, I'll expect you to show some respect to your confessor and some genuine contrition for the mockery you just made of a holy sacrament.'

'But... but I... I didn't,' I stammered.

'Go on now, get out,' the priest snapped, 'before I come around there and give you a clip round the ear. You should be ashamed of yourself. Ghost stories in the confessional! I've never heard such blasphemy in all my life. I've a good mind to...'

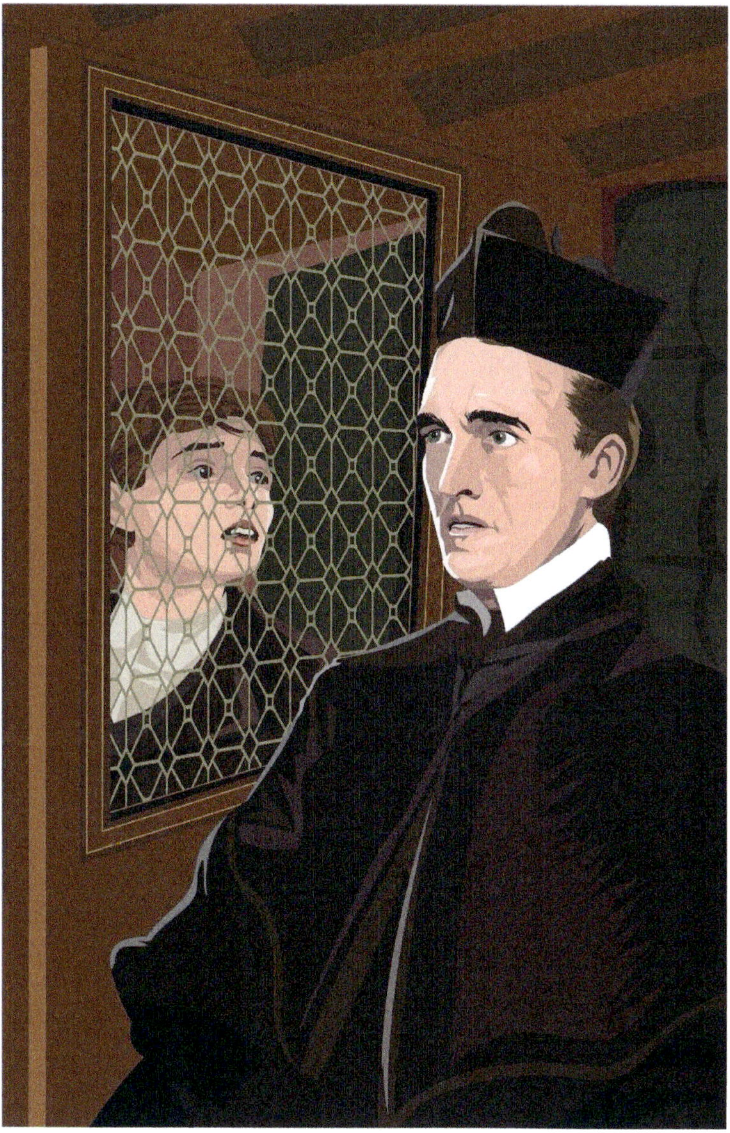

I fairly sprinted out of the church that day and, truth be told, never again went back to confession while that particular priest was on duty. But if I had expected that unexpected scolding to be the end of the matter, I was to be sorely mistaken for, the following Sunday, immediately after the eleven o'clock mass, I saw that very priest making a beeline for my mother.

My heart was in my mouth, I don't mind telling you. Terrified of what would happen if he told her of our encounter, I watched anxiously from a distance. Surely he wasn't about to break the sacred seal of the confessional?

'Do you have something you want to tell me?' my mother asked suddenly as we made our way home.

'No,' I said. 'Why?'

'You know why,' she said. 'You saw me

talking to the priest or, rather, being lectured by him.'

'That's against the law,' I spat back. 'He's not supposed to tell what's said in confession.'

'And he didn't,' said my mother. 'At least not exactly. All he said was that if my son ever decided to use the confessional to play practical jokes again, he would make sure that the boy would be read from the altar at the next Sunday mass. Now, I'm going to ask you again. Is there something you want to tell me, or would you rather tell it to your father?'

'No, don't,' I pleaded. 'Don't tell him. He'll go nuts. I'll tell you, but you have to promise not to laugh.'

'Oh I don't think I'll be laughing,' she said, 'with the new priest threatening to shame us in front of the entire parish. What exactly have you gone and done?'

And that was how I came to tell the story to

my mother.

My mother listened intently, with an ever-creasing brow and an increasingly heavy heart. When I'd finished, she put a consoling hand to my face and sighed.

'You poor thing,' she said, at length. 'Your uncle Albie had the same affliction. He could see spirits too.'

I have to admit, this was not the reaction I had been expecting and it threw me somewhat. I didn't quite know what to say. A sense of relief washed over me and, I'm not ashamed to admit, I came over quite emotional.

'Used to talk about the things they'd tell him all the time, did Albie,' my mother went on, drawing me closer as she spoke. 'Hadn't an ounce of sense. People became frightened of him and, though he wouldn't harm a fly, he still ended up being put in St. Ita's. The poor man was kept there till he died.'

'I don't remember an Uncle Albie,' I said. 'Did I ever meet him?'

'No, son, I'm ashamed to say you did not,' my mother sighed. 'I know it's only down the road, but I could never bring myself to set foot in the place. Now, listen very carefully. You must never tell another living soul about what you saw that day, or speak about any other ghosts that you might happen to see going forward. Understand?'

I could see the fear in her eyes and, though I didn't fully understand what she meant, I nodded. She could tell I was confused.

'People get very frightened of those that see and hear things that nobody else can,' she explained. 'So if you don't want to end up like your uncle Albie, then you'll have to keep such things to yourself. If the confession thing comes up again, just say that it was only a joke; that you just wanted to see the look on the priest's face. Okay?'

'Okay,' I said uncertainly.

'Then promise me now, on your mother's life, that this will remain our secret. That you will never mention it, or anything like it, to anyone ever again.'

'I promise,' I said, and this time I meant it. But somewhere deep down inside of me I already knew that the keeping of a promise could prove a far harder task than the making of one.

To be fair, I *did* manage to keep that promise for a long time and have lived contentedly for many years under the false assumption that Daw would eventually appear to someone else and that this other person would help him instead.

A couple of years ago, however, like Joseph Daw himself, I happened to witness something that changed my mind. It was a Friday evening and I was driving home from visiting a friend up in Ballyboughal. As I passed over Daw's bridge, I caught sight of a young man standing there with a camera.

Now, as you probably know only too well, there is very little worth photographing at that bridge, and so the presence of a photographer intrigued me. I should probably have parked the car on Turvey Avenue and walked back to speak with him, but I didn't.

But then, later that same night, it suddenly occurred to me that maybe the young man had seen something that he, too, couldn't quite believe and had returned with his camera to try and capture it. I know that if I had come across Joseph Daw in his gibbet today, I would probably do just that, if only to prove to myself, and others, that I hadn't been imagining things.

But I guess a part of me didn't want to know.

You can understand that, right? I had never fulfilled my promise to Joseph Daw, and I still felt a little guilty about that. In fact, I have never stopped having the occasional dream about the afternoon that I met him, and whenever I do I inevitably wake in a cold sweat. Guilt never leaves you, you see. No matter how hard you try to bury it, it keeps bobbing back to the surface.

Of course, by telling you all this now, I am breaking yet another promise – the one I made to my mother, and I can't help feeling just a little guilty about that too. But I am an old man now. My days are numbered. I don't want to arrive in the afterlife to find that Joseph Daw is still stranded between this world and the next and his continuing limbo is partly my fault.

And so, should it happen to pass that one of you should grow up to become an historian, or even an archaeologist for that matter, perhaps you will remember the story of Joseph Daw and use your advanced education and professional skills to discover what has happened to his bones.

And if, by some remote chance, you should happen to come across them lying forgotten in the dusty drawer of some old museum or laboratory, then perhaps you will also be decent enough to see to it that the poor man finally gets the kind of decent burial that he craves – the kind of Christian burial that will finally allow him to join his parents in the afterlife.

But if not, and you are fated to live the same common-or-garden type of life that I have, then perhaps you will simply remember the story of poor Joseph when next you cross Daw's Bridge and share it with others.

That, at least, would be something. Every

child should know the history and traditions of the place they grow up in and, like it or not, Joseph Daw, and the Turvey murders, are very much a part of that history.

Appendix

THE REAL JOSEPH DAW

THE MURDER OF Barnaby Sherwin and his family at Turvey in Donabate was widely reported in the newspapers of 1770. The reason for the murders, however, was never reported or discovered. That was a secret that Joseph Daw took with him to his grave.

But people always want answers and, when answers cannot be found, people will inevitably create their own. And that is exactly what happened to the story of Joseph Daw, after whom Daw's Bridge in Donabate is named. What people didn't know, they made up and these made-up details were passed on to subsequent generations, who then invented details of their own.

The legend of Joseph Daw has been told around Fingal for centuries, and in particular around the townland of Turvey, the place where the murders had taken place. While researching this book I have been told, and have read, many versions of this legend, not all of which agree on important details.

Some versions began with a patch of red grass that was said to have been the point where Daw cleaned his bloodstained knife. Others began with a tree upon which a leaf never grew. Some said that it was his wife and daughter that Daw killed, others his adoptive family. Some of them told of a deliberate shipwrecking.

In this novel, I have combined and enhanced the best of these stories with as much historical detail as I could find, but this book is still a work of fiction, a retelling, if you like, of a popular legend. It is not a report of the actual facts of the case.

The actual story of Joseph Daw probably lies buried in the gap between the folklore and the court reports of the day, but after two hundred and fifty years, the truth of the matter may never be fully known. As each generation added their own embellishments to the gaps in the story, a legend was born, and for centuries the true story of the Turvey murders was all but forgotten.

All that changed, however, in 1933, when a bank of the Ballough River[1] collapsed on the Lusk side of Daw's Bridge about halfway between Turvey Hill and Blake's Cross on the old Drogheda Road.

---

[1] Also variously known as the Corduff River, Ballough Stream/River, or Nine-Stream River

The collapsed riverbank revealed what was originally thought to have been part of a suit of armour, and rumours quickly spread of the discovery of a Viking warrior. Archaeologists were called in to investigate, and further digging revealed the body of a man in a gibbet – an iron cage in which the bodies of executed prisoners were hung to discourage others from criminal activity.

This form of execution was occasionally used in eighteenth and early nineteenth-century Ireland in cases of piracy or other serious crimes. Commonly known as being 'hung in chains' or 'hung in irons', such executions traditionally took place at, or close to, the scene of the actual crime for which the man had been hanged.

Under the Murder Act of 1752, the body of a convicted murderer could not be buried unless it had first been sent to a medical school to be

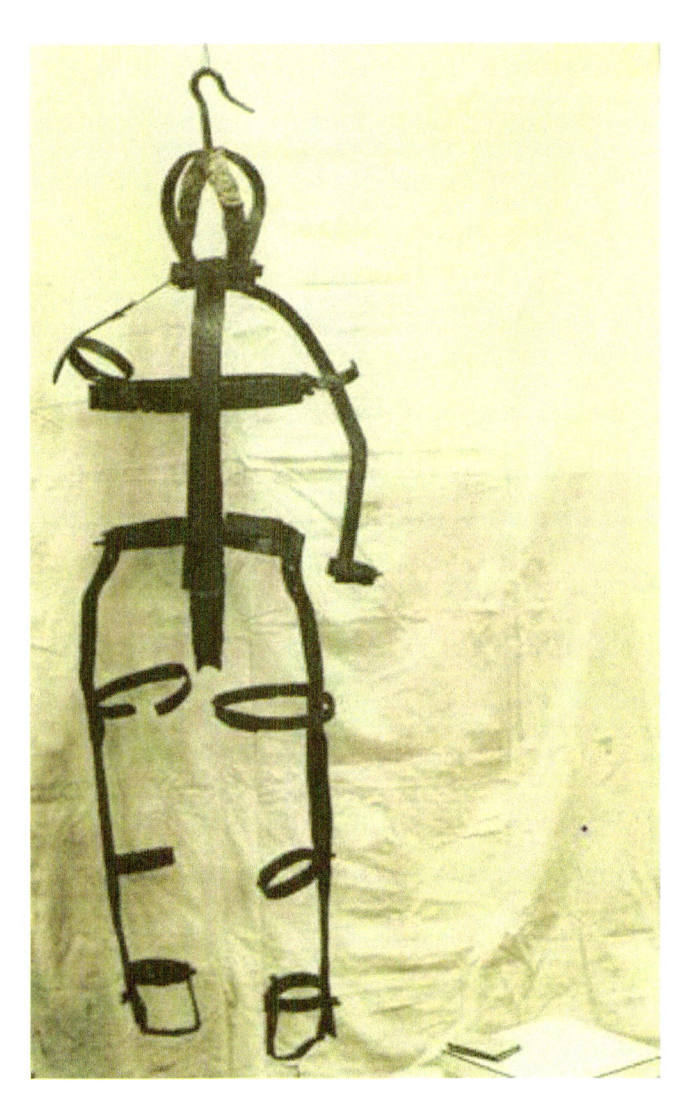

Gibbet used in St. Vadier near Quebec in 1763.
Photograph courtesy of New York Public Library.

practised on by medical students, or it had been turned over to the Sheriff to be hung thirty feet in the air in an iron gibbet as a deterrent to would-be criminals.

You may well have seen gibbets in such popular movies as *Robin Hood Prince of Thieves* (1991) or *Pirates of the Caribbean – The Curse of the Black Pearl* (2003). You may even have seen them used as Halloween decorations, or come across them in any number of historical novels. If you have, you might be surprised to learn that the use of such devices was not very common, and was reserved for only the most brutal of murders, or murders in which there was an exceptional public interest.

The gibbet discovered at Daw's Bridge in Donabate, therefore, was so rare a find that it was reportedly taken to the National Museum, and the skeleton that lay within it sent to the

Daw's Bridge today. Photo © Gerard Ronan

Anthropology Department of University College Dublin. However, there is no record of the gibbet in the records of the National Museum, so it seems likely that it was in too poor a state to be conserved.

The discovery, nevertheless, revived a certain interest in the legend of Joseph Daw and several historians began searching for details of his case. In various newspaper archives from September of 1770, they found reports of his trial, most especially in the pages of the *Freeman's Journal* and the *Leinster Journal*.

According to these reports, the murders had taken place at about 9 pm on the night of 8 September 1770, at Turvey, in Donabate. They were, by all accounts, the result of an especially frenzied attack. Three men were, at different times, arrested for the crime, namely John Ryan, John Farrell, and Joseph Daw. All three were sent to Newgate Prison to await trial.

Having confessed to having falsely accused both Ryan and Farrell of involvement in the murders, and to having committed the murders himself, Daw was subsequently tried and found guilty of the Turvey murders. According to the *Leinster Journal*, he was ordered upon sentencing to be taken back to Turvey and there to be 'hanged in irons. He received his death sentence, it was widely reported, 'with resignation'.

According to the *General Newsletter* of 15 May 1771, Daw's remains had hung in gibbets at Turvey for almost seven months before being taken down, on 11 May of that same year, following the intervention of a Catholic priest.

This priest, apparently, had spotted Daw's remains hanging from a tree while passing on the Newry to Dublin stagecoach. He was, it was reported, so outraged by the barbaric scene, that he ordered the coachman to stop.

In those days the gibbeted bodies of executed prisoners could remain hanging in their place of execution for years, sometimes even for decades. No one would dare to cut them down as it was a criminal offence to interfere with them.

Nevertheless, upon the priest's instruction, the body of Joseph Daw *was* taken down and buried in a shallow grave by two local farmhands. And there, close to the bridge that would eventually bear his name, the body of Joseph Daw lay in an unmarked grave, until 1933, when it was finally revealed by a collapsing riverbank.

Where the bones of Joseph Daw lie today, is anybody's guess, but it is unlikely they are marked by any kind of headstone or buried on consecrated ground. To this day his only memorial remains the stone bridge that traditionally, if not officially, bears his name. Whether that is appropriate or not, is for you to decide.

SMUGGLING IN PORTRANE

Various, but by no means all versions of the legend of Joseph Daw, revolve around the story of a deliberate ship-wrecking. But while the practice of luring ships to their destruction was often alleged to be common practice in places like Cornwall and Connemara, there is no official record of any deliberate shipwrecking ever having taken place at Portrane.

The practice of luring ships to their destruction using false lights has long been a part of maritime folklore, but it is unlikely to have ever happened or to have worked in practice. Sailors were always more likely to assume an unidentified light to be coming from a house on land than from another ship.

The light from a ship's lantern, furthermore, was unlikely to travel very far at night. Indeed various tests have shown that a ship would have to have been within 200m of a single candle lantern before they would even become aware of it.

Having said all that, stories of false lights and 'stalking horses' had become so widespread by the eighteenth century, that people genuinely believed the practice to be widespread. In 1735, this mistaken belief even led to the passing of a law making the hanging of false lights a criminal offence. Not a single person, however, was ever prosecuted under this statute.

Nevertheless, with stories of false lights

having become so tightly woven into the fabric of maritime folklore, it was perhaps inevitable that the people of a coastal peninsula would eventually incorporate such details into the telling of their own myths and legends. That is often the way of it with folklore, old stories become entangled and embellished with the passing of time.

But if the matter of shipwrecking was unlikely to have ever happened, smuggling was another matter entirely. Indeed the entire coastline from Skerries to Malahide was notorious for the practice as there were simply far too many coves and inlets to be adequately policed by customs officials.

The centre of the smuggling trade in eighteenth-century Fingal was the coastal town of Rush, whose sheltered harbour provided a base of operations for such famous smugglers as Luke Ryan, Thomas and Joseph

Rickard, Robert Burnet, John McCarthy, and many others.

When smuggling eventually became unprofitable, many of the smugglers began to turn to privateering, or state-sponsored piracy, and sailed most frequently under French protection or 'letters of marque'.

The practice of privateering, however, turned a previously peaceful Fingal smuggling community into a body of battle-hardened veterans. And so, when the smuggling trade eventually resumed, it did so in the context of a greatly altered atmosphere and became an increasingly violent and dangerous activity.

But while the centre of smuggling operations was generally centred around the harbour at Rush, the people of Portrane and Donabate were also heavily involved, even if the local member of parliament, George Evans (in whose memory the iconic Round Tower at

Portrane was built), was inclined to blame everything on his neighbours on the northern shores of the Rogerstown Estuary.

In 1771, for example, less than a year after the execution of Joseph Daw, and while his remains were still hanging in irons close to the bridge that would eventually bear his name, the excise men confiscated a hoard of seventy-five chests and twenty casks of tea, and no less than one hundred and eleven casks of brandy in a single seizure at Portrane. On the same night, over at 'The Island' in Donabate, eight hundred casks of tea and brandy were seized.

So organised were the smugglers reported to have been, that a barn in Donabate, to which the revenue officials had taken the confiscated goods, was reportedly besieged by up to five hundred armed men wearing white cockades in their hats.

Even allowing for some exaggeration, such

numbers would appear to suggest that smuggling was very much a part of the local culture and local economy in 18th century Fingal.

CHILD KIDNAPPING IN IRELAND

DURING THE EIGHTEENTH and nineteenth centuries, Irish children between the ages of three and six were frequently kidnapped and sold into servitude. The trade was cruel, organised, and highly profitable. Indeed, it was so profitable that, in 1781, one woman admitted to having received as much as £30 from a ship's captain in return for supplying him with children. That would be the equivalent of more than €6000 in today's money.

Many, though not all, of these kidnapped

children, were sent to be sold into indentured servitude in America (a form of slavery in which the child would work, not for money, but to repay a set sum, such as the alleged cost of their purchase). Other children were taken to be used as climbing boys by chimney sweeps, or to be used by farmers as farm boys. Still more were taken by street gangs to be horribly maimed and set to beg.

As clothing was expensive in the eighteenth century, there was also a thriving market amongst the poor for second-hand clothes. Children, especially wealthy children, were frequently kidnapped for their clothes, and then abandoned naked in the streets. It was not until 1815 that a law was passed increasing the sentence for 'child stripping' to seven years transportation to the penal colonies in Australia.

By 1819 the practice of child stripping had

died out. Child kidnapping, however, continued to be a problem, and stories of an adult, usually a woman, luring young children away with fruit, sweets, gingerbread, or the promise of a toy, were quite common at the time.

A blind eye was often turned by the rich to the kidnapping of poor children, and the failure of parliament to provide a specific penalty for child kidnapping often meant that those caught in the act were dealt with more harshly by the communities from which the children had been taken than by the police.

So widespread was the practice that, on just a single day, namely 28 April 1781, the *Freeman's Journal* reported no less than four separate incidents of child kidnapping in Dublin. In one of these, a woman was caught in Thomas Street, Dublin, luring five children away with gingerbread cakes. Caught by an angry local mob, the woman was stripped, dragged about the streets, and had her ears cut off.

Under torture, this woman confessed to having kidnapped twenty-seven other children during the previous fortnight. She also gave her captors the address of a house on the Liffey quays from which the children were eventually rescued.

On that very same day, another woman was arrested on Crane Lane, off Dublin's Dame Street, with two kidnapped children in her possession. In return for not being punished, she, too, gave the police the address of a house, this time on Barrack Street[2], from which a further eighteen children would be rescued.

Child kidnapping and child slavery did not die out in Ireland until the 1840s. But it was

---

[2] Now part of Benburb Street.

not the opposition of Irish politicians that finally put an end to the trade, rather the collapse of the international market for child slaves following the abolition of slavery and indentured servitude in America.

ACKNOWLEDGEMENTS

I am indebted to Zoe Stephenson for her editorial assistance and advice, and to Una Walshe and her 6th class students at Scoil Phádraic Cailíní for having test-read an early draft of the book. Many thanks are also due to Derry Dillon for his wonderful illustrations, and to Marcel Koortzen for proofreading the finished work.

Special thanks are due to Helen O'Donnell, Betty Boardman, and the staff of the County Archives in Fingal County Council, for their continued support over several years now, of my efforts to document many of the lives and legends of the Portrane Peninsula. And finally, I owe a debt of gratitude to my wife, Cliona, and daughter, Eleanor, for their continued forbearance and support.

TALES OF OLD TURVEY

OTHER BOOKS
IN THE SAME SERIES

The Legend of Gobán

GERARD RONAN

Illustrated by Derry Dillon

Born in Turvey, near Donabate, in north County Dublin, Gobán Saor was the greatest craftsman and builder in Ireland. But he was also, reputedly, one of the smartest Irishmen who ever lived. Long after his buildings had been forgotten, people still told fireside stories of his gripping adventures and the clever ways he outsmarted his enemies.

The Old Man and the Tower

GERARD RONAN

Illustrated by Derry Dillon

Twelve-year-old Rufus has been disqualified from a National Short Story competition. The judges have accused him of copying the story of a child who won the competition twelve years earlier. But Rufus's story was not a work of fiction. It was a true account of his encounters with a mysterious old man who spoke in riddles – a man who had taken to hanging about the Martello Tower in Donabate the previous summer.

But how could that be? How could two children have shared an identical experience twelve years apart? And why did they both choose to write about it? And why, when the two eventually meet, will the encounter change both of their lives forever?

Lucky Kate

GERARD RONAN

Illustrated by Derry Dillon

Orphaned and homeless at the age of sixteen, Kate Ryan is sent to the county workhouse at Balrothery where, after three years of picking oakum, she is offered the opportunity of a lifetime.

To save on the cost of caring for them, the workhouse guardians are offering to pay the passage of three young women to the new colonies in Australia, where there is a shortage of women. Tickets have already been booked for them on the largest passenger ship ever built – the *Tayleur*. It is a voyage that will change Kate's life forever.

Printed in Great Britain
by Amazon